FAIRY TALE CLASSICS

Aladdin

tiger tales

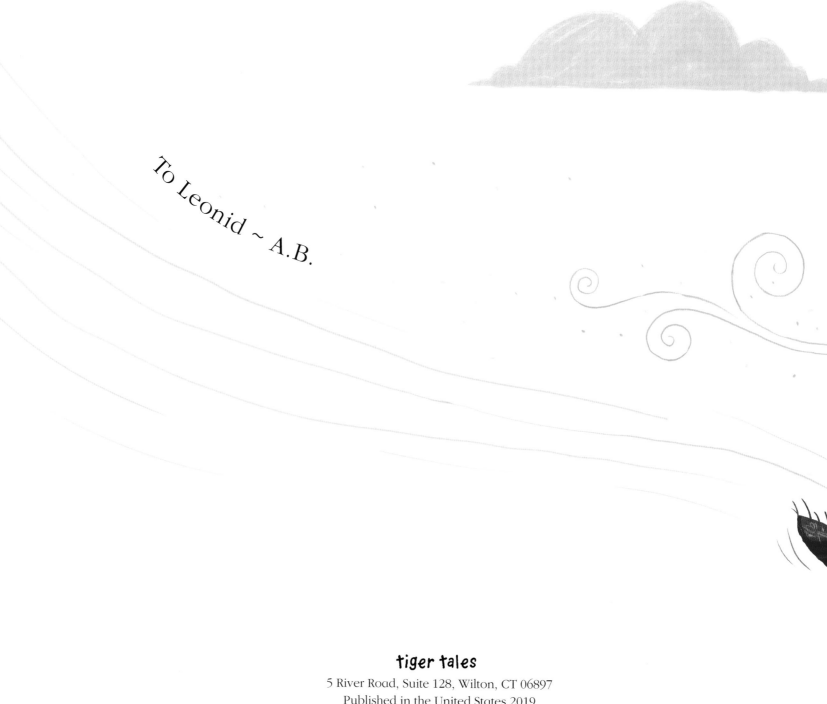

To Leonid ~ A.B.

tiger tales

5 River Road, Suite 128, Wilton, CT 06897
Published in the United States 2019
Originally published in Great Britain 2019
by Little Tiger Press Ltd.
Text adapted by Anna Bowles
Text copyright © 2019 Anna Bowles
Illustrations copyright © 2019 Shahar Kober
ISBN-13: 978-1-68010-135-5
ISBN-10: 1-68010-135-8
Printed in China
LTP/1400/2380/1018

For more insight and activities, visit us at www.tigertalesbooks.com

FAIRY TALE CLASSICS

Aladdin

adapted by *Anna Bowles*

Illustrated by Shahar Kober

tiger tales

Aladdin was a clever boy who lived with his mother.
One day, a stranger knocked on their door.
"I'm your long-lost uncle," he said. "And I'm a magician.
I have a job for you that will make us rich!"

Aladdin's mother didn't remember having a brother. But she was definitely tired of being poor. So she let Aladdin go.

"We're going to find a valuable lamp!" said the magician.

In a cave?

Be quiet. And start crawling!

Aladdin
squirmed
through tiny
tunnels. Soon he
saw a golden lamp.

"Bring the lamp
to me!" bellowed the
magician. But the lamp
was so beautiful that
Aladdin wanted to keep it.
The angry magician
blocked the entrance.
There was no escape!

Aladdin hugged the lamp tightly, rubbing it with his hand.

Then something wonderful happened!

Smoke swirled from the genie's fingers. When it cleared, Aladdin was standing in a city street.

Right in front of him was the sultan's daughter, Princess Bala! "I shouldn't be here," said Aladdin. "And you *definitely* shouldn't be here."

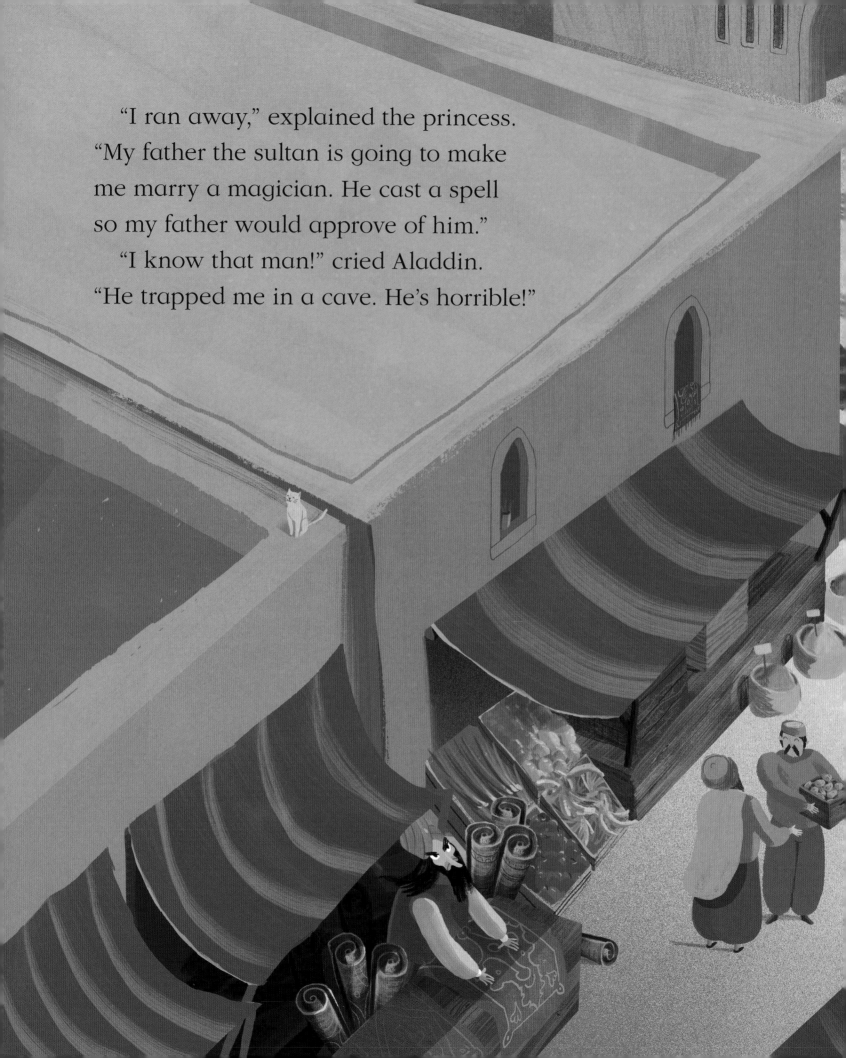

"I ran away," explained the princess. "My father the sultan is going to make me marry a magician. He cast a spell so my father would approve of him."

"I know that man!" cried Aladdin. "He trapped me in a cave. He's horrible!"

Aladdin and Bala took a magic carpet ride together far above the city and told each other about their troubles. Bala said, "Come to the palace tomorrow. We'll try to reason with my father."

But the next day, as Aladdin walked to the palace, the magician caught him and pushed him into the river. Aladdin frantically rubbed the lamp.

"Your wish is my . . . ,"
began the genie.

Quick! I wish I
was on dry land.

Then the genie said,
"Listen. This is important. Your
wish isn't *always* my command.
You only have a total of three wishes."

Meanwhile, inside the palace, the magician was trying everything to make Bala love him.

He gave her flowers.

He wrote her poetry.
(It was awful.)

Finally, he
cast a spell on her.

Aladdin returned and tried to break the spell.
He waved a hand in front of her face. He kissed her cheek.

Then he had an idea. He caught the magician's stinky breath in a bottle and had Bala smell it.

"Ugh!" she cried, and the spell was broken.

But while Aladdin was helping Bala, the magician snatched the lamp and rubbed it.

"Your wish is . . . ," said the genie.

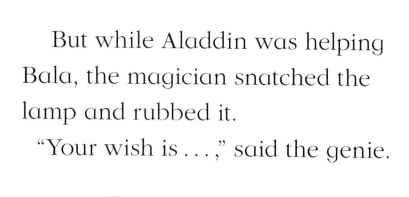

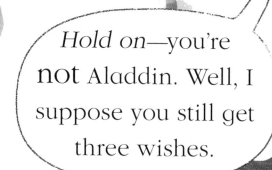

Hold on—you're **not** Aladdin. Well, I suppose you still get three wishes.

The evil man cried, "I wish to be the world's most powerful magician! I wish I was in charge instead of the sultan!"

When the smoke
cleared, they
were all in the
throne room.

"My third wish is to make Bala love me," said the magician.

The genie refused! "No way! I can move stuff around, but I can't force people to feel things. Rules are rules."

The magician stomped his
feet and shouted in rage.

Bala crept up behind the magician. But just before she could grab the lamp, he spun around and seized her. He cast a terrible spell. Bala found herself trapped in an hourglass!

"Admit you love me and I'll let you go!" the magician promised.

Never. Ever.

Ever

EVER

EVER!

The magician had had enough!
"This is ridiculous!" he cried. "I wish I was a genie and didn't have to bother with any of you . . . .

Oh . . . dear . . . I just used my final wish!"

The genie was very happy to grant the magician's third wish. There was a dramatic swoosh, and the magician ended up inside a rusty old lamp.

When the magician was gone, the hourglass shattered. Bala was free!

"If only I was a prince, then I could marry you," said Aladdin.

"So use your third wish!" said Bala.

"I can't," Aladdin sighed. "I need that for something else. Genie, I wish you were free!"

The delighted genie flowed out of his lamp and disappeared.

Bala turned to the sultan. "See! Aladdin is brave *and* kind. You must let me marry him."

Aladdin and Bala were married that very afternoon. They lived happily ever after—in their very own way.

Anna Bowles

Anna is a writer and editor of children's books who has
adapted several fairy tales for the Fairy Tale Classics series.
She lives in London, England, with her husband, her collection
of fluffy hippos, her books, and a large supply of chocolate.
If she was a fairy tale character, she would probably
be the trombone player from the Fairy Tale Classics title
Beauty and the Beast.

Shahar Kober

Shahar is an illustrator who works from a very small studio,
in a very small town, in a very small country. When he's not drawing,
he enjoys taking care of his very small garden with
his not-so-small children.